CAN MAN

KILLER OF COP-KILLERS

BOOK TWO

A NOVELLA BY JOHN DITTO

ISBN: 978-0-578-49970-3

email: canman@reagan.com

Acknowledgments

Thanks to my sister, Denise Ditto Satterfield, Author of *The Tooth Collector Fairies Series www.toothcollectorfairies.com*

Police Officer Luke (Chad) Branton for buying the very first book of this series.

And special thanks to Linda, Mona, Sara, Morgan, Miguel, and Todd.

Introduction

In Book Two of the Can Man series, Jack finds himself searching for another cop killer with no clues to go on.

Chapter One

Jack couldn't figure it out. He was lying next to his beautiful girlfriend, Heather, that he met a few months ago. He owned a profitable pub that catered to local police departments, and lots of those cops were his good friends. He should have a smile on his face from ear to ear, but he didn't. Jack wasn't sure if it was his heart or his mind, but he still had deep feelings about his deceased wife Suzanna, who was murdered in a bank robbery. He still had that feeling - the one that drove him to hunt down killers of cops and kill them. He'd use his custom made knife.

Officer Stevens who died that day trying to protect his pregnant wife, never leaves his thoughts. When the night came, Jack could don his Can Man disguise and move around by tightrope roof top to roof top watching over cops that were out on their beats. Jack also liked the quietness of the late nights. Since he owned a pub, he didn't have to wake up early for some 9 to 5 job. He could sleep in. Just as long as he could get his pub open by noon for his day time regulars. They were mostly older, retired construction workers.

Friendships had developed there, so if Jack was 10 minutes late, he'd never hear the end of it. Jack laughed to himself. If these guys were told that their friend and pub owner, Jack Warren, was also Can Man killer of cop killers, they would laugh and say you're crazy. That was the way Jack wanted to keep it. Jack got himself up, did some sit-ups and push-ups before hopping into the shower. After getting dressed he was ready for another day of running his pub, Suzanna's Pub. He arrived at 11:40 AM and some of his regulars were already waiting outside. One of his regulars was Big Don who stood about 6'5" and had a light gray beard. He always sported the same look– blue jeans, cowboy boots and a pearl snapped button shirt. He carried a small ice chest in his truck, filled with his favorite beer. He and some of his buddies didn't have to wait till Jack opened his Pub but, Jack had a rule. No one could bring their beers in when the pub opened. Jack opened the front door and his daytime regulars followed him in. His routine was to turn off the alarm, turn on the lights and wait on the regulars. The day was going along as any other day.

Heather was at the beer delivery company working the phones while he took care of his pub. Four o'clock rolled around. Jack knew his regular cop customers would start coming in soon. His daytime customers were already gone. Sergeant Mike and Officer Gorby were the first cops to come in. Twenty minutes later Chief Dickens entered and sat down with Sergeant Mike and Officer Gorby at the bar in their usual spot. All the flat screens were on with the sports network giving all the scores from the previous night. Jack walked over with a bar towel, shining up a beer mug. The four talked a little bit.

Sergeant Mike turned to Jack and said, "We were just talking about Chief Dickens retiring this summer. We want to have his going into retirement party here at Suzanna's."

Jack gave a big smile and said, "I'd be honored to have it here at Suzanna's Pub."

Sergeant Mike said, "Good. Then it's settled. We'll have it right here." The Sergeant turned to Chief Dickens and said, "Do you think you can find the place okay, Chief?"

Dickens immediately responded, "Shut up, Mike!" They all laughed.

At six o'clock the three cops paid their tabs and headed towards the door. It was dusk outside and Jack followed them out. He wanted to thank them again for choosing his pub for the Chief's upcoming retirement party. They stood around in a circle out on the sidewalk just to one side of the front door. Officer Gorby was saying something about the chief retiring when he stopped speaking in mid-sentence. Jack looked over at him. Gorby's eyes were gone and light was coming through his eye sockets. He dropped like a sack of potatoes. Chief Dickens screamed, "Sniper!" Everyone hit the deck. Jack backed into his brick entrance and peeked around the edge. He saw nothing but old brick buildings all the way down the street.

Cops in the pub raced toward the door with pistols drawn. Chief Dickens ordered, "Stay inside."

Jack looked down at Officer Gorby. He had a half inch circular hole at the bridge of his nose. Everything behind his forehead was gone. The only thing that could cause this kind of damage was a very large caliber sniper rifle.

The sun was completely down now and it was dark outside. Cop cars filled the street. Red and blue flashing lights bounced off of the buildings. The street was blocked off. The police began a building to building search for the sniper. Everyone knew that he was long gone. They found nothing. The sniper wasn't stupid. He picked up his spent shell and took off.

The detectives came out to do a trajectory analysis. They stood where Gorby was and approximately where the bridge of his nose would have been. They went to where the bullet impacted the sidewalk, about 20 feet further down. With a laser they could back track the bullets path. It went six blocks down to across the street and up an old brick four story warehouse rooftop. They figured that is where the sniper was perched.

The large caliber bullet traveled at almost 3000 feet per second. When it hit Officer Gorby, the kinetic energy was too great for his head to contain. It just exploded outward. It was a horrible sight. The three were debriefed by detectives but there really wasn't much they could tell. It happened so quickly. Chief Dickens and Sergeant Mike were busy telling lower ranked officers what to do and where to go. Cops kept asking Jack if he was all right. He kept reassuring them that he was okay, but Jack had already gone into Can Man mode. He was already thinking like a killer of cop killers.

Chapter Two

As the night wore on, cop cars started moving away to go back on their assigned areas to patrol. The waitresses, Betsy and Jolene, were told they could leave. Jack was finally able to close the pub and go home.

Heather came over that night but all he could do was think about what had happened. How could he find the sniper cop killer before the cops? He knew they would be in full search and arrest mode.

The next morning before getting ready for work Heather nudged Jack. "Are you alright?"

Jack opened his eyes and said, "No, I'm not alright, but I'll be okay."

He looked down and then back up again and said to Heather, "I'm sorry I'm acting like this, but I want you to know that I love you so much. Thank you for your understanding and putting up with me."

Heather smiled and said, "And thank you for putting up with me." Before leaving for work she hugged him and said, "You are my best friend that I will love forever."

When Jack drove up to the pub he spotted yellow crime scene tape everywhere. Detectives were taking pictures, measurements and making notes. Officer Gorby's remains had been removed yesterday. The sidewalk washed and cleaned.

Jack entered his pub. The place looked normal. It was the horror that occurred just outside his front door that everyone was concerned with, but Jack did have a pub to run. He was a couple of hours early. There was no rush.

Jack unlocked the front door and stuck his head out through the yellow tape and asked a detective, "When do you think you guys will be finished?"

The detective walked over and said, "Hey Jack. Should be out of here in about another hour."

Jack thanked him and shut the door. Someone knocked on the glass front door. Jack turned back around and saw the detective wanted to say something more.

Opening the door the detective leaned in and said, "We at the station are sorry this happened here at your pub and we are still going to come here like before. We are not going to let some murderer with a rifle frighten us to not going where we want to go!"

Jack shook his hand and thanked him for his and the station's support.

Eleven o'clock rolled around, the yellow tape was gone, and the last police car pulled out. That was a good thing. Jack didn't like his pub being a crime scene. He knew the press was going to descend on him after he opened. Nothing he could do about that. They had a job to do, just like him.

At a quarter till twelve his regulars started to gather outside. Jack was glad that the murder didn't scare them away. Local TV news trucks were there, too. You know the kind with the giant dish on top of their van and their TV station logo painted on the side. Jack took a deep breath and opened the front door.

The regulars rushed in first followed by the press with microphones in hand. Jack announced that he would speak to the press after he served all of his regulars. Each time he gave them a beer they shook his hand told him that they were sorry about what happened. Jack thanked them for their support.

Jack then turned his attention to the reporters that were patiently waiting over in the table area. He didn't want to be rude, but the sooner they were gone, the sooner things could get back to normal. As he walked up to them, cameras with high powered lights came on.

Reporters with microphones leaned into him. And they all wanted to ask the same questions, "Are you okay? Did you see the shooter? Was anyone else hurt? And, who do you think did this?"

Jack fielded the questions as best he could. He held up his hand and said, "That's all for now." He was trying to wrap it up.

Some reporters wanted to talk to the daytime regulars, but they had no interest in talking. None of them were there when it all happened anyway. Jack made his way back behind the bar and put a sports game on all the TVs. Every news channel was reporting on the murder at his pub. All Jack wanted was days to pass and they find something else to talk about.

Late afternoon was approaching and his first police customers should have begun to file in. It was 6 PM and still no cops. All the daytime customers were gone. For the first time since Jack opened his pub, he was alone in the early evening. He called both waitresses and told them to take the night off.

Sitting on a barstool, thoughts of what all had happened in the last 24 hours were almost overwhelming. Jack was trying to put things into some kind of order of importance. He thought, *find the sniper first, take care of Heather, and take care of business*.

Sergeant Mike had already said that he suspected Jack was the Can Man. That meant even more carefulness in the search for the sniper. Two more days went by without a single cop coming in. Jack was now starting to worry about his business. On the third day around 4 PM, Chief Dickens and Sergeant Mike came in and sat at their usual barstools in front of the TV.

Jack went over with the biggest smile and shook their hands. "I was starting to think the worst."

Chief Dickens said, "Out of respect for Officer Gorby, I told the men to stay away from here till he was buried."

Jack replied, "I understand."

Chief Dickens got up and went to the restroom.

Sergeant Mike looked at Jack and said, "If there was some way I could speak to Can Man, as a friend, I would tell him not to do anything regarding the sniper. We can handle it and take care of it ourselves."

Jack replied," If I could, I would tell him that for you but I don't know him and also I agree that you don't need his help. You can handle this yourselves. Please arrest this cowardly murderer as soon as you can and of course stay safe."

Sergeant Mike thanked Jack for the kind words, picked up his beer and leaned back for the last swallow. About then Chief Dickens returned to his stool. The two men paid their tabs and left.

For a moment Jack wondered if Sergeant Mike had mentioned to anyone that he suspected he was also the Can Man. Probably not. Next thing to do is very quietly start gathering info on the sniper. Listening to the cop chatter at his pub was his usual source of info. But if he could somehow learn what the detectives knew, that would be huge. But that's not how things work. Detectives ask questions, not give info.

Chapter Three

Later on in the week Jolene brought in a new friend she met at the junior college. They were both wearing jeans with colorful t-shirts. Jolene said, "This is my friend Maria."

Maria was about 5 foot seven, slender, with shoulder length dark hair, and a pretty smile. She shook Jack's hand and said, "It's very nice to meet you." Her dark eyes were a little intense.

Jack replied, "Welcome to Suzanna's Pub." Jolene said, "Maria's looking for a job."

Jack looked at Maria and said, "Well, I wish you luck. But right now I don't need any more help."

Maria said, "That's okay. There were plenty of jobs posted at the school."

"Well, keep her in mind if something comes up," Jolene said. "We'll see you later Jack." "It was nice meeting you," Maria said.

Jack went back to running his pub. The sniper was really the only thing on his mind.

Whoever this guy was, he was very good. Chief Dickens told Jack the shot came from about a half a dozen blocks away. The shooter was in an elevated position. This meant that this guy was probably military, and a champion sharpshooter. He used a large caliber rifle with powerful scope.

That evening when Jack got home he went online to look up the best snipers in the U.S. Military. He knew it was a longshot and thought, *no pun intended*, but it was a starting point.

After about an hour nobody look promising as the sniper. It was puzzling to him that a champion sniper would want to kill a cop. This was a tough one. It just didn't make any sense. Jack hopped into bed and called it a night.

A week passed and everything was getting back to routine. Officer Gorby was buried and people were talking about him less and less.

Jack shined up glasses as he walked back-and-forth behind the bar. He listened closely to cop conversations for updates on the sniper. In the background, Jack overheard a sports caster on the local news channel say something about an athlete thinking outside the box. He stopped pacing and stared at nothing, thinking about what he just heard. Thinking outside the box. Maybe that's why nothing he tried made any sense. The sniper didn't have to be military. Heck for that matter, the sniper didn't even have to be an American.

Jack really started to rethink everything. The bad news was now he didn't even know where to begin his search. The facts were that the killer was a very talented marksman able to make an incredible shot at a huge distance. The bullet slug was never found. All they had was the chipped cement sidewalk where the slug impacted. That's all there was to go on.

Saturday night at the pub had been a busy one. After closing, Jolene and Betsy were both sitting down and resting their feet. They both made good tips that night. The pub was closed and Jack was doing his usual cleaning. Betsy's boyfriend knocked at the front door to pick her up. Jack unlocked it to let her out. About 15 minutes later Jolene left. Jack locked the door behind her and went back to wiping down the bar. Nothing worse than a sticky bar.

As Jack ran his fingers down the bar checking for spots that might've been missed, he heard loud screams from the side parking lot. He grabbed his pistol from a drawer behind the bar and unlocked the door and ran to the parking lot. He thought to himself as he ran, *please don't be Jolene. Please don't be Jolene.*

In the dimly lit parking lot he saw a woman lying on the ground. *Oh no*, he thought to himself. It was Jolene. He knelt down and placed his hand on her shoulder. She looked up at Jack and threw her arms around his neck. Jolene was crying and shaking. After helping her up, they made their way back into the pub.

"What happened," Jack asked?

"I was going to my car when all of a sudden somebody from behind me grabbed my hair and pulled me down backwards." After catching her breath again, Jolene continued. "This bum looking guy stole my purse and told me to shut up."

She lowered her head into her hands and said, "All that work, $211 and my driver's license, credit cards, and keys, all gone."

Jack got up. When he and came back he handed her $211 out of the cash register. Jolene said, "Jack, I can't accept this money."

Jack said, "Take it. It will make me feel better."

Jolene cracked a smile and said, "Okay, only if it makes you feel better."

"Okay, first things first," Jack said as he took over the situation. "Start calling your credit card companies to do some cancelling and I'm going to call my Locksmith buddy to come over here and make you a new key for your car. Then he will follow you home and make one for your front door."

Luckily, Jolene had her cell phone in her pocket and didn't lose it when the attack happened. Also she already had most of her credit card customer service numbers. They were both on the phone when there came a very loud knock at the front door. Jack could see it was Officer Garza. He let him in.

Garza said, "I heard a scream. I was only a block and a half away walking my beat. What the heck happened?"

Jack filled him in. Officer Garza called EMS to come out and check on Jolene to make sure she was okay.

Jack saw yellow caution tape everywhere. He thought to himself, *not again.* In the last two weeks he had police investigations going on at his pub. Jack walked over to one of the cops holding a clipboard.

"How long is this going to take?" Jack asked.

The cop responded. "We are almost done here and I'm glad the young lady wasn't hurt too bad. We will be completely gone in about a half hour, tape and all."

Jack was relieved. He walked over to where the paramedics were putting a bandage on Jolene's forehead.

About that time Maria pulled up in her old pickup truck. She ran over to Jolene and gave her a big hug. Jack thought, *good she's got her friend here*. As the last cop left and Jack was alone in his pub he thought about Jolene's attacker. She said he was a bum looking guy. She described him as about 6'1"and wearing an old coat that had some red plaid design. Good information. Even though the Can Man is not in the business of catching muggers, the police are.

Jack went home and put on his nocturnal outfit and tight roped his way to the building tops. It was a clear night and he could use his night vision binoculars and see everything. As he was looking down at the streets, there were a few people leaving the local bars. Several homeless people were in the alleys going through the trash cans and dumpsters. These were sights he'd seen many times, but none of them fit the description of Jolene's attacker.

Jack knew the night cops usual beat and decided to go over a few buildings to where Garza should be. Sure enough there he was doing his checking front doors on all the closed businesses and looking inside their front windows for anything out of the ordinary. Jack scanned up three or four blocks in front and behind officer Garza. It looked pretty clear, no one to be seen. Tilting his head up skyward towards the stars, Jack thought about Officer Gorby's killer. *Not much to go on.*

About then came a little noise down below. Jack was perched on the three-story building. It was low enough to hear noises on the quiet streets late at night. No cars or trucks driving around. At first he couldn't see anything so he walked around the perimeter of the building. Not making a sound and listening for more noise to direct his attention to see who's down there. Being perfectly still, the noise came again. It wasn't in the alley, it was in one of the recessed front door entrances of a shop. Jack couldn't get a clear look so he quickly and quietly tightroped over to the two story building across the street. Now, he had a very nice view of the stores' front doors.

Using the night vision, the dark entryways became visible. *Not in that one. Not in that one. Hello*, Jack thought to himself. He spotted someone. He had his back to the street and he was wearing a plaid jacket. *Wow, is this Jolene's mugge*r? Jack thought.

Suzanna's pub was about six blocks away. *Patience*, he thought. *Patience*. After waiting a few minutes, the bum threw something down. Zooming in with the binoculars, Jack could see it was a purse. Officer Garza was about a block away. He needed to somehow direct Garza to the mugger.

Jack scaled to the alley down below and cut through to the next block. Officer Garza was across the street checking front doors. Jack found an empty soda bottle. He moved to about the halfway mark of the long alley. Crouching down against the wall he rolled the soda bottle. It made enough noise to be heard in the quiet of the night.

Jack pulled in the slats of his Can Man outfit and now he looked just like a trash can in the alley against the wall. Peeking through the slit of the slightly open lid, sure enough it was Officer Garza in the alley with his flashlight illuminating his way. Jack eased the lid all the way down and listened. The footsteps went right past him. Jack loved his costume. It was like he was invisible.

Raising the lid a little bit, he watched Officer Garza walking out the other end of the alley. Jack thought, *Okay, Jolene's mugger is in the doorway on the left, don't turn right.* So, of course, Garza turned right. Scrambling up a fire escape Jack stood on top of the three-story building looking down to about where the mugger was hiding. Reaching into his pocket he pulled out some loose change. He fished out a couple of coins and drop them down below.

They noisily hit the sidewalk.

Garza spun around and started briskly walking towards the sound. Jack watched as he approached the mugger, pistol drawn. The suspect had no interest in trying to escape.

After putting the cuffs on him Garza picked up the purse and radioed in for a unit to come pick up the suspect and haul him to jail. The police car was there in minutes. Jack patted himself on the back and was glad he could help.

Back at the station Officer Garza found Jolene's info in the purse. He asked the suspect if he had mugged a lady earlier and took her purse.

Looking up with a smart aleck grin he said, "I don't know what you're talking about." That purse was just lying on the street. A call was made to Jolene's cell phone for her to come down to the station.

In the meantime, Sergeant Mike got some police officers to put on their regular clothes to stand in a lineup. Jolene and her new friend, Maria, arrived shortly later. As the men were walking out in the lineup, Jolene pointed out her attacker before they even reached their spaces. Sergeant Mike asked number three to step forward and turn around.

"That's the guy, that's the guy," Jolene said.

After all the excitement was over, Jack worked his way back to his apartment. He was glad that Jolene's attacker was caught. He could now turn his attention back to the sniper. Nothing but blanks kept coming up. Time for sleep.

Chapter Four

At the station, Sergeant Mike was interviewing the suspect. The guy was a career lowlife criminal, full of attitude. After growing tired of giving the guy the chance to confess, Sergeant Mike told him he was already identified by the victim and he was found with her purse. After locking him up Sergeant Mike was about to walk away when he turned and said to the suspect, "You are such an idiot. Officer Garza said, 'If you hadn't made all that noise with the bottle and then drop some change, you probably wouldn't have been caught.'"

The suspect looked up from behind the bars and said, "I didn't make any noise with the bottle and I sure didn't drop any change. The loose change went it in my pocket."

The Sergeant looked at him one last time and said, "And you're a terrible liar, too." He locked the second barred door and left. He said goodbye to a couple of cops and got in his car to drive home. There were no cars on the street which allowed him to time think as he drove. He laughed to himself and thought that if this guy would just confess, the DA and the judge will go easier on him. Also, the guy wouldn't even admit he made all that noise that directed Officer Garza to him. The sergeant stopped at a red light, and when it turned green, his own lightbulb went on. Maybe he wasn't lying. Maybe someone else made those noises that directed Garza to the suspect. Of course, it was Can Man. Mike smiled and said to himself under his breath, thanks Can Man for that one. And you didn't even break any laws. The sergeant laughed out loud in his car.

The next day at the pub everything was normal. The daytime regulars didn't even know that there was a mugging the night before in the parking lot. About 4 o'clock Jolene walked in the front door. Jack met her at the bar and told her she could take some time off if she wanted.

Jolene smiled at Jack and said, "I'm fine and I want to work. I just feel silly with this big bandage on my fore head."

She handed Jack the $211 he gave her the night before.

He put up his hands and said, "No, that's yours even though you were able to get everything back. Consider it a gift from Suzanna's after all you went through."

Jolene got a little misty eyed, hugged Jack, then whispered in his ear, "You are the best boss. Thank you."

He looked her in the eyes and told her, "I'm making some changes around here. The parking lot is getting a bunch of new lighting. I'm also having security cameras installed outside with a monitor here behind the bar.

Then I'll be able to see you make it safely to your car."

Jolene laughed, "You would think a pub full of cops would be the safest place in town."

Jack nodded and agreed. "Yes, I think it is, but sometimes there is one idiot that is just too dumb to realize that."

They both went back to work, Jack tending the bar and Jolene checking on customers at the tables. All of the daytime regulars were gone and the off-duty police were starting to file in. Amongst them was Sergeant Mike. Only this time he came in alone. Which was odd Jack thought. He always comes in with one of his buddies from the station. Mike sat at his usual spot in front of the TV at the bar. Jack poured his regular draft beer and walked down to serve him.

The Sergeant looked up at Jack and said, "I like you, Jack, and I like your pub."

"Well thank you", Jack muttered."

Then added, "I would like to also thank you for coming to Suzanna's Pub. Plus, you guys did a great job last night finding and arresting Jolene's attacker. She was so happy to get all of her stuff and money back. I offered to give her some time off, but she wouldn't take it."

Sergeant Mike responded, "Well, we love her down at the station and are glad that she is okay. As a matter of fact we took up a collection just to help her out."

The Sergeant handed Jack a fat envelope. "Wow, there's a lot of money here. Hold on."

Jack called Jolene over. She walked up with her tray, smiling with a big bandage on her forehead. "Yes, what's up," she asked looking at both of them.

The Sergeant held out the envelope.

Jolene opened it and was truly surprised. Getting misty eyed she said. "I don't know what to say. But thank you so much, you didn't have to do this."

Mike told her it was all the guys at the station.

Jolene sat her tray down and gave Sergeant Mike the biggest hug. Then she wentbehind the bar, opened the cabinet door, pulled out her purse and put the envelope in. Walking back to pick up her tray, she smiled at both of them, "You guys are too much, thanks again."

Mike looked at Jack and asked, "Why is she thanking you?" Jack responded, "I gave her a couple of hundred dollars." "That was very nice of you." The sergeant said.

Jack told Mike about all the upgrades he was doing to make the parking lot a lot safer. "Better lighting and security cameras."

That's a smart idea," said the Sergeant, "You know if more businesses did that, it would slow down crime and it would aid us when there is video to review."

Mike leaned forward and said in a lowered voice, "Those noises that lead Officer Garza to the suspect were pretty instrumental in catching that guy. And if I were a betting man, I'd say it was our nocturnal friend Can Man. And before you say anything, I for one would like to thank him." The sergeant leaned back, crossed his arms and smiled.

Jack said, "Me too. If that's what happened. Glad he was out there." Both men seemed pleased.

Jack worked his way back down the bar serving customers and cleaning glasses. More officers poured in along with Chief Dickens. Every bar stool was taken. Jack thought to himself, *this is great. This is the way it should always be. Yeah right.* He laughed to himself.

Jack kept his ears open trying to pick up any news on the sniper. All night and all those cops, not one word. Then it dawned on him. Maybe they had been told not to speak about the investigation. Well heck. Now what am I supposed to do?

About that time Heather walked in. She was so pretty half the guys stop talking. She made her way over to the bar. They gave each other a little kiss.

Jack said, "I'd offer you a seat but the bar is full."

Heather responded, "I see that. What a great problem. I'm coming back there to help you."

Jack said, "No, no, you can't do that. You're my girlfriend. I'm not supposed to ask you to help me here at the bar."

Heather answered, "You didn't ask me. I volunteered. Besides, if I wash up glasses it will free you up to take care of customers."

He thought, that's hard to argue with. He handed her an apron and Heather went right to work removing empty glasses and wiping the bar down. If that wasn't enough she picked up a plastic bin and went out to the tables removing empty glasses. Jolene and Betsy were grateful for the extra help.

Closing time finally came. As Jack locked the front door, all four of them flopped down at a table. They were pooped.

Jolene said, "It's funny how just sitting down could feel so good." Everyone nodded yes.

Heather looked at Jolene and said,"I hate to pry, but what happened to your forehead?"

"No, you're not prying. I've only been asked about 100 times tonight. Last night there was a burning building and I caught a baby falling out." Everyone laughed.

"Just kidding, I actually got mugged last night."

"Oh my God!" Heather said.

Jolene continued, "It's Okay. I wasn't seriously hurt and the bad guy was caught. I even got my purse and everything in it back." Everyone clapped.

About that time a knocking at the front door. Jack jumped up to see who it was. It was Jolene's new friend, Maria. Jack unlocked the door and let her in. He led her over to the table and pulled her up a chair. Everybody said hello.

After about a half an hour Jack's stood up and announced it was late and time to lock up. He got no arguments as all of them were tired.

Heather stayed at Jack's apartment that night. So, no nocturnal activities for Can Man which was fine because Jack was physically exhausted. But not too tired to be with his girlfriend Heather.

Chapter 5

The next few weeks pasted uneventfully. Jack was starting to wonder if Officer Gorby's murder was a one-time thing. Maybe it was a hit on him instead of law enforcement officers. Still so little to go on.

The bar phone rang.

"Hello, Suzanna's Pub." Jack answered.

It was Heather. He looked up at the clock. It read almost 3 o'clock.

She said, "Something terrible has happened. Another police officer has been shot. And the radio said it was a sniper."

Jack looked down and shouted, "No!"

He thanked Heather for the call, even though it was very bad news. "I'll call you later after work tonight," he said.

Jack walked over to one of the bar TV's and put it on the local news.

A reporter was on the scene. "A cowardly act just happened earlier today. An officer just got into his personal pick-up truck at the Porter police station, when a bullet smashed his windshield.

Officer Morrison was grazed on the side of his head. He was rushed to the hospital where his condition is listed as guarded. And he should make a full recovery."

Jack was grateful that the officer was going to be okay. Now, Jack needed to get his focus back on the pub. His regulars should start filing in pretty soon.

Once again Jack would pace the bar up and down trying to pick up some chatter on the Porter police station sniper. As usual, Chief

Dickens and Sergeant Mike were the first two cops to arrive.

Pouring both of their favorite beers, Jack met them at their usual sitting spots in front of the TV. Leaving the news station on might provoke them to talk about the attempted capital murder.

The sergeant looked up at the TV and asked an open question, "What's the world coming to? This guy works all day protecting people and then some psycho tries to kill him, getting into his pick-up truck."

Chief Dickens answered. "It never makes any sense. All we can do is catch him before anyone else gets hurt or worse."

Jack and Sergeant Mike agreed.

Walking back down the bar, thinking to himself, it's too early for any info. It just happened. And the only thing I can come up with is to think outside the box. And that's a big area.

More off-duty officer's started filing in. Also Jolene and Betsy arrived. Those two waitresses know the ropes and went right to work. Jolene's forehead bandage was smaller. That was a good sign. Maybe that will mean less questions about the burning building. Jack's smiled to himself.

That evening around closing time, Maria came into the pub. Jolene told Jack that they were going out clubbing. The pub closed at 10 PM so there was plenty of time for those two to go out. Maria was dressed in a black T-shirt, camo pants and desert storm like boots.

Jack thought to himself, *times have really changed. Whatever happened to the little black cocktail dress?*

Time passed without any new info on the sniper. All Jack learned was that the detectives figured out where the sniper was positioned. No bullet casings were found, no nothing. They took the trajectory of the bullets path and worked their way backwards. It led to a vacant four story building roof top six blocks away. The sniper really had some talent to strike a moving target at that distance. Jack thought of the similarities to Officer Gorby's murder. The sniper was located on a rooftop of a vacant building. It was dusk and both victims were cops. In neither incident was the bullet located or the shell casing found.

All he knew was that the sniper liked rooftops and darkness – just like the Can Man. The thing is rooftops don't have people to see you and there are no security cameras. If there are any cameras, they are pointed down not towards the roof. But a mental image was starting to form. To run up and down all those stairs meant that the sniper was young and fit. Had perfect vision and is a very skillful Marksman.

Jack had a mental image of what the sniper looked like. But the big question was why would a skillful sniper want to kill cops? There must be an explanation. Somewhere, somehow, something happen to set this guy off. *You must be stopped,* Jack thought.

The next few days brought no new news. Porter, Texas was too far for Jack to do his night time activities. He had pretty much decided that he was just going to put all of his efforts into protecting his local station police officers. And that was big enough job for Can Man to handle.

Jolene was very capable of running the pub on Sundays. Business was slow and allowed Jack to take a day off. And that was perfect because Heather was off on the weekends. They decided to go to the city park where the police department had their barbecue and that's also where their relationship started. Once again it felt good to be in the park with the fresh air and sunshine. This brought a calm and peace to Jack when he was with Heather.

He told her, "I really don't realize how wound up and tense I am till I come out here with you.

Thank you Heather for getting me to relax and smell the roses. You know, I used to own a flower shop."

They both laughed. It was getting late and the sun was starting to go down. As they were holding hands and walking back to their car,

Jack had a flash thought that this is the time of day when the sniper attacks. Right before sunset. Jack even looked up to the rooftops across the street from the park. Nothing to see. As Heather was getting into the passenger seat, Jack was loading their picnic stuff into the trunk of the car. As Jack slammed the trunk lid shut there came a loud gunshot. It echoed off of the buildings. Jack immediately ducked down and moved to Heather's door. Opening it, he took her hand and let her out to duck behind the car. Heather was not panicking. Jack was protecting her with his body. No more shots were fired. As they stood up, they saw some people moving towards the intersection one block away. A police car was blocking traffic on one side.

Jack looked at Heather and said, "I'm taking you home right now. You'll be safe there." She asked, "What about you?"

Jack smiled and said, "Don't worry about me, I'll be fine."

After dropping off Heather, he raced back and found a parking spot a few blocks away from the shooting. Walking up to the scene there were about a dozen patrol cars, police redirecting traffic and yellow tape everywhere. Jack could see a police cruiser in the middle of the street with a shattered rear window. Looking up the street behind the car were lots of buildings with mid- rise rooftops. Exactly the same as the first two sniper attacks. Looking over the chaotic scene Jack spotted Chris, the first cop's life he saved while being disguised as the Can Man. Officer Chris Morgan walked over. He knew Jack from his pub not knowing he was also the Can Man.

Jack spoke first, "What happened here?"

Chris pointed over to the damaged police car and said, "Apparently someone shot at the Police cruiser from behind. The bullet missed Officer Alford by inches." He pointed up the street. "It came from one of those buildings."

Jack patted Officer Morgan's back and said, "I am glad you are okay. Stay safe." Jack walked a little closer to the disabled cruiser and saw the broken rear window.

He thought himself, *Thank goodness Officer Morgan is okay. This was a new one. The sniper tried to shoot a cop while he was still inside his car. And no silencer this time. Maybe the sniper wanted to scare the people also. It's almost as if the sniper is challenging himself with a harder shot.*

Jack looked up. He thought he saw Maria on the other side of the street. With the light fading and all of the onlookers, he couldn't be sure. It did look like she had on those camo pants and a black T- shirt. But Jack couldn't be sure. He lost sight of her in the crowd.

Monday at in Suzanna's Pub, Jack learned several things. He heard that this sniper had drawn the attention of a number of Law Enforcement Agencies, state police, FBI, ATF and several local police departments. They were determined to get the sniper fast.

Chapter 6

It was later in the week when Maria came by at closing to pick up Jolene. The two of them were going out for cocktails.

Jack let her in. He said, "Hello. How are you doing?"

Maria responded, "I'm doing fine and I found a job waitressing at the coffee shop just off campus."

Jack said, "That's great! Hey, I wanted to ask you a question. Was that you I saw the other day where that police car was shot?"

"Nope, Not me." Maria answered.

Jolene told Jack, "We are out of here. Time for someone to fix me a drink!" They all laughed.

After Jack locked the door behind them, he walked back and sat on a barstool. He was thinking that it sure looked like Maria but it was getting dark and it was across the street in a crowd of people.

Back at the station the detectives found the slug in the police car. It was pretty mangled but intact. They sent it to the FBI lab for testing and identification. It turned out that the slug is from a foreign weapon. Probably Russian. And it was a big caliber. Exact identification wasn't possible because of the condition of the slug and there were some pieces missing. But the detectives were glad to have something from the sniper. Jack and law-enforcement still were no closer to finding the sniper.

A few weeks went by without the sniper attacking again. Maybe there was too much heat from the police. And Jack discovered that many of his tight ropes had been removed. He figured, with so much investigating of rooftops, that somebody noticed them and took them down. He didn't think they knew that they were being used as tight ropes to get around on. Now, he would just use his disguise to help him move around and he would stay on the ground. After a few nights he realized how much he relied on those tight ropes. Not to mention his viewpoint from up high.

It had been about a month without any sign of the sniper and law-enforcement had returned to their regular routines. Jack decided to re-install a few tight ropes to see if they would be noticed. A week or so went by and they were still there. Jack thought, *that's great.* He began putting them back up everywhere and discovered that some buildings still has the original tight ropes in place. He really liked having the ropes back. Now he had that great advantage point to see up and down the streets at a far greater distance. Jack was still trying to figure out how to find the sniper. He thought to himself, *think outside the box.* Now he wasn't even sure what that meant.

It was midweek around 3:30 PM that was the time when the early regulars have left and the cops haven't started coming in yet. Jack was watching one of the flat screens when a woman's archery tournament came on. It was amazing how these women could hit a bull's-eye that far away with the arrow. The commentator was talking about how archery doesn't require great strength. But it does require a good eye and excellent aim.

Jack went back to wiping down his bar. *No sticky spots,* he laughed to himself. He wondered if he was some sort of a neat freak. Swirling the damp towel around all of a sudden he froze. Looking up at the TV, the commentator was saying something about how these women could shoot the middle of a playing card at 50 yards. *Now wait just a minute. Could the sniper be a female?* Jack ask himself. *Wow, now that's really thinking outside the box.* Nobody was looking for female sniper. He stopped wiping down the bar and watched the rest of the archery tournament.

Four o'clock hit and the show was over. A commercial came on and in walked Sergeant Mike and Chief Dickens. Quickly taking care of them, Jack walked back to the other end of the bar to think about his new theory.

Jolene and Betsy filed in right on time. Jack was so excited that he might be onto something. He was glad the girls were there.

Jack said, "Jolene. Can you watch the bar for a minute?" She responded, "No problem."

Jack went into his little bar office to get online to investigate female snipers. Turns out there are very few, if any, in the US military. However, Jack learned that some Middle Eastern countries have female snipers in their ranks. Very interesting Jack thought to himself. That bullet the detectives retrieved was Foreign, maybe Russian. Some Middle Eastern armies use Russian weapons. *Could it be a female sniper from a foreign country with a grudge with the police?* Jack asked himself. All of a sudden he felt he was back in the game and ahead of law enforcement.

Moving fast on this idea was important. The police detectives are not stupid and could very well figure out what Jack just did. The bigger question was could Jack kill a female cop killer? It took about two seconds for that answer. Yes he could. She needs to be stopped. Jack almost said it out loud.

Jack returned to the bar feeling a new surge of energy. If Jack was right, she had already killed one cop, wounded one and barely missed another. Thinking outside the box had paid off. All he could do was check roof tops at dusk. But how long could he make up excuses to leave his pub to go run an errand at sunset.

That night at closing Jack and the girls were sitting at one of the tables after the last customer left. Jolene said she and Maria were going to a carnival that was in town.

Jack said, "Have a great time and bring back a large stuffed animal."

Jolene laughed and said, "Will do."

About that time there was a tapping on the glass front door.

Jack got up. It was Maria. Jack let her in.

"You want a beer?" Jack asked.

Maria said, "No thanks. The carnival closes at midnight and we've got to go."

Jolene jumped up and waved goodbye to Jack and Betsy. Before Jack could close the door, Betsy's boyfriend showed up to take her home. Jack locked the front door and closed up the pub.

Going home he was excited about getting out on his new tight ropes and checking on his police doing their beat down below. While up there on the roof he looked into the night heavens and wondered how to catch the sniper. This shooter was not stupid. Snipers in the military are taught to be unpredictable. They move after every shot. This way another sniper won't be able to locate them and pick them off. The sniper Jack was looking for was also unpredictable, never attacking in the same location. One shot was in the city striking officer Gorby in front of the pub. The second happened weeks later in a small town about 25 miles away, in a police station parking lot. The third happened a month later. The sniper tried to shoot a cop and his patrol car. So this sniper was mixing it up pretty good.

Except for one thing. Two of the three shots fired happened near or at Jack's pub. That meanth that the area might be in the snipers backyard.

Jack worked his way back home and called it a night. Now that he had an idea of who the sniper could be he felt like he was making some progress.

As time passed it started getting closer to Chief Dickens retirement party. Since the party was going to be at Suzanna's pub, there were a lot of preparations to be done. Jack had talk to Sergeant Mike about the decorations and was told that some of the police officers wives would take care of that. All Jack had to do was make sure the pub was fully stocked with beer. The place is going to be at full capacity.

Chapter 7

That night Can Man was tight roping from building to building checking on the beat cops down below. It was quiet as usual. Looking up at the stars he began to think about the sniper. He or she had done some research. The shooting in front of his pub meant that the sniper had already scouted out a vantage point for that shot. And probably had the escape route all mapped out. Jack thought, *is it possible that I've already met the shooter and don't know it.*

The next evening at closing time Jolene told Jack that she had a surprise for him. Jack asked, "What is it?"

Jolene replied, "You'll just have to wait."

A knock came at the front door. It was Maria. Jack opened the door and said, "Come on in."

Maria was holding a large leaf bag. She walked over to Jolene and in unison they said, "Here's your surprise!"

Jack opened up the giant plastic bag and pulled out the largest stuffed pink teddy bear he had ever seen. They all asked what Jack thought about his new surprise.

Jack laughed and said, "Well I have to say this is the largest pink teddy bear I've ever seen. Guess I'm going to have to make a place for it here in the pub."

Jolene said, "We are glad you like it."

Jack hugged them both. "Where did you get the bear from?" he asked.

"Maria and I won it last night at the carnival. Remember you told us to bring you back a large stuffed animal."

"Oh yeah, you're right." Jack said. "I did say that. But I was joking. It's very hard to win anything at those carnivals. All the games are rigged in their favor."

Jolene smiled. "You are right unless you have a sharpshooter friend like I do. Maria couldn't miss."

Jack looked at Maria and thought, *no, no, it couldn't be her. Could it?*

He hugged them both one more time. When he hugged Maria he wondered, *am I hugging and a cop killer?*

That night going to his computer Jack started to research the heck out of Maria. He learned from Jolene that her last name was Farha. She moved here from Cleveland. After checking newspaper clippings and other databases he found a trove of information on her. And it was all bad. She was originally from the Middle East. She had been in the military. She won lots of sharpshooting medals and she had been on numerous missions. It was never mentioned that she was a sniper, but it was possible.

Wow, could Maria be the sniper? Jack had to slow his mind down. This is a big decision and he must be 100% sure. No jumping to conclusions. Just being a female sharpshooter does not make her a cop killer. There has to be a motive. A big one. Jack decided to call it a night and get some rest.

The next day when Jolene came in Jack had some questions about Maria. But he didn't want to tip his hand that he suspected Maria. When Jack was wiping down the bar Jolene came over to order a couple of draft beers. While filling the mugs Jack looked at Jolene and said, "That was really nice of you and Maria to give me that giant bear."

"Of course," she said. "We thought that would make you laugh.

"By the way," Jack asked, "Do you know why Maria moved here?"

"Something happened to her boyfriend," she said. "He died. She wanted to move someplace new and start over."

"That's terrible. How did he die?" Jack asked.

Looking down Jolene said, "I've asked Maria that question, but she just says that she doesn't want to talk about it. OK got to go. People are waiting for their beers."

Jack thought, *That's interesting that her boyfriend died and she didn't want to talk about it.* More research was needed.

Chief Dickens retirement party was approaching fast. As a matter of fact it was this Friday. Just two days away. Everything had taken a backseat lately – the retirement party, the pub and even Heather. Jack was concentrating his attention on finding a motive for Maria to be his cop killer. And nothing seemed to be answering his questions.

Jack was feeling at a dead end that night when Jolene came over to fill an order.

"Jack," said Jolene. "I asked Maria one more time what happened to her boyfriend, and she finally told me. He was shot dead."

Jack said, "That's terrible. How did it happen?"

Jolene leaned over the bar and whispered to Jack, " The police shot him. Apparently he had a gun and was shooting at cars from an overpass.

The police cornered him and told him to drop the gun. And this is where things get murky. The police said he pointed his gun at them and they shot him dead in a hail of bullets. But some bystanders said he dropped his gun and they shot him anyway."

Jack asked, "No video to prove it one way or the other, right?"

Jolene said, "Correct. I've got to get back to my customers." Jolene walked away. Jack was thinking this could be the motive he had been looking for.

The next night was the retirement party. Jack's walk-in cooler was filled to the ceiling with beer. The police officer's wives were coming at around 3 o'clock to do the decorating. That was perfect timing because the early regulars should be gone by then.

The day of the party arrived. When the ladies finished decorating the place, Jack thought it looked so festive that maybe he should just leave the decorations up. He laughed to himself.

It was around 4 o'clock when Betsy's boyfriend dropped her off. Like clockwork Maria dropped off Jolene. Jack thought she used to drive her own car, but after the mugging, I guess she felt safer having someone pick her up. As Maria was about to drive off, Jack waved goodbye to her. He froze. His hands stop waving in mid-air. Oh no. Maria was wearing a black T-shirt and camo pants. The same outfit that she had on when the other two police officers were shot at. Could that be her sniper uniform? Maria shouted to Jack that she was going to park her car down the street and would be right back. Jack thought that was good. He could keep an eye her.

The wives were the first to get to the pub. He guessed that they wanted to make sure everything was ready for the big retirement party. Jolene, Betsy and Maria were also busy helping the policemen's wives. As the wall clock approached 5 o'clock policemen started filing in. Jack started wishing he had a bigger pub. He knew that this night was going to be standing room only. Shortly thereafter, Chief Dickens entered with Sergeant Mike and Officer Garcia. Immediately, everyone clapped and started singing, *for he's a jolly good fellow.*

Jack welcomed everyone to Susanna's pub for the happy occasion. The chief was in good spirits and all the off-duty police were patting him on the back and wishing him a happy retirement. The pub was now completely full.

Officer Garza walked over to Jack and said, "I can't stay because my shift starts in about 10 minutes. I can't even have a beer."

Jack shook his hand and said he understood. Officer Garza turned to leave. Jack told him, "The next time you come in, your first two beers are on the house." Garza laughed and shook his hand and then left.

Jack made his way over to the man of the hour, Chief Dickens, and said, "Well Chief, I am really happy for your retirement and I hope you get a lot of fishing in."

Chief Dickens and smiled and shook Jack's hand. "I'm really going to miss the station and all the great men and women that work there. Thirty-five years just flew by."

The chief grabbed his mug and clanged it with a small flashlight he had with him. Everybody stopped talking to listen. The chief spoke to the standing room only crowd.

"I just want to thank each and every one of you for coming out to my retirement party. And I also want you to all know that it was my pleasure working with you for the past thirty-five years."He paused then said, "Well most of you." Everyone laughed and clapped. "And I have an announcement. After speaking to the mayor, we have both agreed that we want to Sergeant Mike promoted to take my place."

Sergeant Mike was in shock at the big promotion that just happened.

The new chief and the old chief shook hands and gave each other a man hug. Everyone was clapping. It was turning out to be quite a wonderful occasion. While Chief Dickens was shaking hands all around, Jack felt a tap in on his shoulder. It was Maria. Jack's big smile and happy face turned a little more serious. He looked at Maria and said, "Yes, what is it?"

Maria was about to speak when Chief Dickens turned around to Jack and said, " Listen Jack, I just want to thank you for hosting this party. I also want to thank you for having this pub for a place for the officers to hang out. And last but not least, I want you to know that just because I'm retiring from the department doesn't mean I'm going to stop coming here."

Jack thanked him and said, "Let me get you a beer."

Chief Dickens put up his hands and answered, "I can't, but thank you so much for everything. I have to leave here in a few minutes. My wife and I are going out to dinner to do some celebrating of our own."

Jack shook his hand one last time and told him he would see him again at the pub. Jack turned around to ask Maria what she wanted but she was nowhere to be seen. Thinking he didn't have time to look for her, he went back behind the bar where there was some room. Jack looked at his full bar. He took out his camera phone, stood on a stool, and took a picture of his packed bar. This was going to be framed and put on the wall. As Jack was looking at the photo he just took he could see both waitresses and many regular police officer customers. He thought good, everyone is in the picture. Then a cold chill went down his spine. Where is Maria?

Chapter 8

Jack looked all around the room, no Maria. "Jolene, have you seen Maria?"

"No I haven't. But I'm sure she is here somewhere. Maybe she's in the restroom."

Jack thought that was a possibility. He made his way to the women's restroom. As he got there, one of the police officers wives was coming out.

Jack asked, "Are you having a good time?"

"Oh yes" She responded. "And thank you for letting us use your pub as a venue for our event." "My pleasure. And by the way, is there anyone left in the restroom?"

She said, "Nope, it's empty."

Jack's mind started racing. Maria was in her camo outfit and missing. Then a terrible thought entered his mind. She was standing there when Chief Dickens said he was leaving. Could she have parked her car down the street to have her sniper rifle right there? Could she be thinking of shooting Chief Dickens as he was leaving the pub – just like what happened to officer Gorby? She could even be in the same spot again. Jack had no time. He raced out of the pub and over a few blocks to his apartment.

He ran upstairs and slung open his cedar chest. He thought, no time for Can Man outfit. He just grabbed his special knife, binoculars, and headed over to that four story building. The one that the detectives figured that shot came from that killed Officer Gorby.

Jack worked his way up the fire escape on the old building. He kept saying to himself, *don't leave yet Dickens*. He neared the roof, he slowed down and didn't make a sound. He could now see the entire roof. Pulling out his binoculars he flipped it over to night vision. Looking down the roof edge he came to the corner of the building. There with her back to him was Maria. She was aiming towards his pub with the biggest rifle he had ever seen. The scope was very large and on the end of the rifle barrel was a long extension. He figured that was a suppressor to keep the noise to a minimum. The weapon had a bipod that rested on the edge of the roof. Maria was looking through the scope and had earplugs in. She didn't want any distractions while aiming. This allowed Jack to move up behind her. He was using his own binoculars to watch his front entrance to the pub. Even though he was now certain Maria was the sniper cop killer, he wanted to wait till Chief Dickens came out.

It was a clear night with a gentle breeze. Maria never took her eye away from the scope. Barely breathing, Jack had his knife ready. He watched his front door area. There appeared the man of the hour. Chief Dickens.

In one swift movement Jack moved towards Maria. Unbeknownst to her the blade was already in front of her throat. Seconds seemed like too much time. Thoughts of his dead wife Susanna, Officer Gorby, and Officer Steven's who gave his life trying to protect his wife, all raced through his mind in pictures. Jack held his breath, then ended the threat. He finally took a deep breath.

Maria's rifle was now pointing up in the air. The extra-long rifle barrel could be seen from the street down below. But it wouldn't be visible until the morning.

Jack made his way to his apartment where he put the special knife and binoculars into the cedar chest. He raced back to the party going on at his pub. Chief Dickens was gone and a few people had left but it was still packed. Jolene was working behind the bar.

Jack said, "Thanks for covering for me. I was talking to the chief outside." Jolene smiled and said her usual, "No problem."

Jack looked up and saw that Heather had arrived. Heather said, "Better late than never."

He was so glad to see her. They hugged across the bar. Heather told Jack that she was here to help. There was no arguing from him. Every glass was out. Heather grabbed a plastic bin and went out to pick up empty glasses.

Jolene came over to Jack and asked, "Have you seen Maria? I've looked everywhere for her?"

Jack said, "No, I haven't see her. My hands have been full just trying to take care of this retirement party. She's your friend. You know her a lot better than me." He smiled to himself.

As the night wore down to an end, Jack shut and locked the front door behind the last customer and gave out a big sigh. "What a night!"

The two waitresses and Heather agreed. They were all sitting around one of the tables trying to catch their breaths. Jolene stood up to make a complementary announcement. "Jack Warren, you really pulled it off. This was a record breaking night for you and the pub. I believe all three of us girls agree that if someone asked if we knew anyone that could have successfully held this huge party, we would have all pointed at you and said, 'he Can...Man.'"